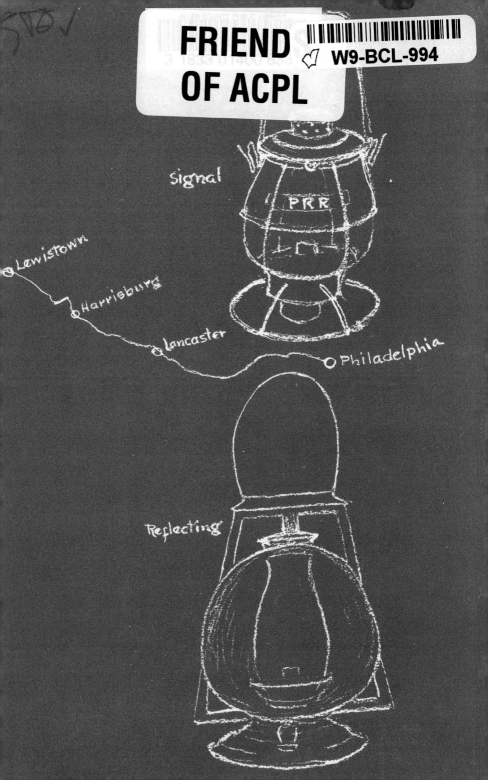

Signal

PRR

Lewistown
Harrisburg
Lancaster
Philadelphia

Reflecting

Whistle For the Crossing

Books by Marguerite de Angeli

BLACK FOX OF LORNE

BOOK OF NURSERY AND MOTHER GOOSE RHYMES

BRIGHT APRIL

BUTTER AT THE OLD PRICE

COPPER-TOED BOOTS

DOOR IN THE WALL: A PLAY

THE DOOR IN THE WALL: STORY OF MEDIEVAL LONDON

ELIN'S AMERIKA

FIDDLESTRINGS

GOOSE GIRL

HENNER'S LYDIA

JARED'S ISLAND

JUST LIKE DAVID

THE LION IN THE BOX

PETITE SUZANNE

POCKET FULL OF POSIES

TED AND NINA STORYBOOK

THEE HANNAH

TURKEY FOR CHRISTMAS

UP THE HILL

WHISTLE FOR THE CROSSING

YONIE WONDERNOSE

WHISTLE
for the
CROSSING

Marguerite de Angeli

DOUBLEDAY & COMPANY, INC.

GARDEN CITY, NEW YORK

Library of Congress Cataloging in Publication Data

De Angeli, Marguerite Lofft, 1889–
Whistle for the crossing.

SUMMARY: A young boy travels with his father,
a railroad engineer, on the first train between
Philadelphia and Pittsburgh.
[1. Railroads—History—Fiction.   2. Pennsyl-
vania—Fiction.   3. United States—Social life and
customs—1783–1865—Fiction]   I. Title.
PZ7.D35Wh   [Fic]
ISBN 0-385-11552-0 Trade
ISBN 0-385-11553-9 Prebound
Library of Congress Catalog Card Number 76–42323

for Clarke and Erna Moore
to whom I am indebted
for the inspiration for this story

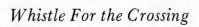

Whistle For the Crossing

1 "School's out! It's over for the sum-m-mer!" Eddie sang out, waving his new certificate saying he had passed into the sixth grade.

"Time for swimming! Time for fun!" Tom tossed his cap into the air in celebration. The cap went so high it caught on a branch of a tree and had to be retrieved, but that was part of the fun. Tom shinnied up the tree after it. The boys were on their way home through the woods along the river.

"D'ya think we can go fishing?" asked Eddie.

"Na-a! Pa had to take the skiff this morning.
Let's hunt treasure in the old ruin, hunh?"

"Do you think there's anything more to find?"

Both boys lived on the banks of the Dela River, but nearly a mile apart in a small scat ing of houses called Penn's Manor, which cluded what had been William Penn's country house, now a ruin. Eddie lived north of it and Tom, to the south.

They came to the fork in the path.

"See you when I have Nellie taken care of!" called Eddie as Tom went on.

"Don't be long!" Tom shouted back.

In this year of 1852, Edward Andrew Moore lived with his father and sister, Lavinia. Their mother had died in the winter after a long illness. Their father, Edward Terhorst Moore, was an engineer on the Camden and Amboy Railroad. He walked the two miles to and from the station where the train stood overnight.

Lavinia, who was older than Edward, had finished Dame school. Plans had been made for her to attend boarding school, but now, since Ma had left them, Lavinia stayed at home to look after Pa and Eddie, cooking the meals and keeping the house neat and tidy. She even did the shopping at the country store.

Next door lived Grandfather and Grandmother

Quinton. They lived with Uncle Steve and Aunt Ellen, Ma's brother and his wife. Grandfather was a conductor on the Camden and Amboy Railroad, and he and Pa usually walked to work together.

There was Meg too, who was only three. Meg was everyone's pet. She followed Lavinia about as she tended the chickens and gathered the eggs. Sometimes she rode on Nellie's back when Eddie led the horse to the pasture. But sometimes, if everyone was busy in the house, Meg wandered off into the woods, or went too near to the river.

Nellie was the mare who pulled the buggy when the family went to church or to market. She dragged the plow when Pa dug up the vegetable garden. She was a useful animal and a friend. Eddie loved her. He kept her coat shining, her stall clean, the manger heaped with fragrant hay, and her bucket filled with water from the pump. This took a lot of time, but when she nuzzled his neck and when Pa put his arm around Eddie's shoulder and said, "You are a good farmer, Eddie. You take good care of our Nellie. I'm proud of you," it was all worth while.

Every so often, it was necessary to take Nellie

to the blacksmith to have a shoe fixed. Eddie loved that. Mr. Lofft, the blacksmith, was just a few miles down the road. He was a pleasant, jovial man who sang at his work.

Eddie liked to watch as Mr. Lofft worked the great bellows with his brawny arms, blowing the fire to white heat and the horseshoe to cherry red. When it was just hot enough, the shoe was hammered into shape on the ringing anvil. How Eddie loved the sound! And the hiss of steam when the shoe was plunged into the water tub to cool. He loved even the smell of the burning hoof as the shoe was fitted!

At first, Eddie thought it might burn the horse's foot, but Mr. Lofft said, "No, no more than it hurts when you cut your fingernails."

There were many sad moments, now that Ma was no longer with them. But Pa tried to spend as much time at home as he could. They missed Ma's presence at meals, they missed her all the time. "Lavinia does her best," Eddie said to himself, "but it isn't quite the way it was when Ma was here. When I came home from school, Ma always had cookies and milk on the kitchen table. Vinny often forgets. Will she remember today?"

As Eddie went into the house he called, "I'm home!" and Vinny answered from upstairs, "Hi, Eddie! Look on the kitchen table. I made some cookies from Ma's recipe." She hadn't forgotten!

"Swell, Vinny!" Eddie answered as soon as he could with his mouth full.

"They're great. As good as Ma's." He went out to the barn to take care of Nellie. She nickered when she saw him coming as if she had been waiting for him. Eddie wrapped his arm around her nose. "Hello, ol' girl," he said, as she nibbled his cheek.

First the water bucket must be filled from the creaky pump. When Nellie had drunk her fill, Eddie shooed her out into the barnyard while he freshened her stall. Gnats and flies swarmed about her in the early June air.

"Take it easy ol' girl till I bring fresh straw." He batted at the stinging creatures, but they only buzzed the louder. Eddie hurried to his work, bringing hay from the loft and spreading fresh straw. He wondered if Pa would come home to-night or if he would have to make that extra run as he did last week.

Leading Nellie back, he watched the move-

ment of her head, the flare of the nostrils, the
flow of the mane. He wished he could draw what
he saw. He had tried often, but what he saw in
his mind was not what came out in the drawings.
Sometimes he didn't hear what people were say-

ing because he was so engrossed drawing in his mind, visualizing the way an ear twists and turns to catch sound, or the way an eye is set in the head. Vinny always encouraged him as Ma had. But Pa said,

"Drawing's all right for fun, but it's a hard way to make a living."

Eddie stroked Nellie's cheek as he slammed the half door and turned the hasp.

He tossed his cap and jacket onto the porch and started to run toward Pennsbury where Tom would be waiting for him.

Just as Eddie started to run, Aunt Ellen's voice called from next door, "EddIE! *ED*W*ARD!*"

"Yes, Aunt Ellen?" he stopped and went back.

"Can you find Meg for me? I've got a cake in the oven and can't leave the kitchen. I've called and called, but I can't find her. Will you please?"

"Sure. I'll look in the woods." He nodded, running on.

There she stood, just in the edge of the woods, watching a squirrel.

"Come now, you little rascal," said Eddie, taking her hand; "your mother wants you." Meg came willingly enough. She was not an unruly child. She was just interested in everything as most children are.

When Meg was safe in her mother's arms, Eddie went on his way. He met Tom halfway to the ruin.

"Where you been? I waited and waited." Tom said, punching Eddie in the ribs.

"Ouch! Take it easy! I had to take care of Nellie, then just as I was leaving, my Aunt Ellen asked me to look for Meg and of course I *had* to."

"Oh, that *girl* again! I walked halfway from Pennsbury to meet you."

"She's not a *girl;* she's only a baby," Eddie said crossly. "Besides, she's my cousin." Eddie had no more interest in girls than Tom had, but Meg was different.

The boys went on through the perfect June day, skipping stones into the river as they neared the bank, chasing squirrels up a tree, scuffing dead leaves. Birds sang declaring their territory, ready for the second nesting. Ed stopped to listen. They seemed to say: "This is m-i-ne!" "Don't come ne-e-ar!" Eddie wished he could draw the rounded throat, the open beak, but the birds were never still. Once, when he found a dead cardinal, Eddie took it home and made a drawing of it, studying its form and how the feathers were set. He marveled at the exquisitely fine barbs that held the feathers in shape. Tom was impatient.

"Come *on!*" he urged. "You going to watch that crazy bird all night?"

Eddie only said, "Look! There's that great old bird that's in my book! I've never seen it before."

"Oh, he's just that ol' woodpecker. He lives around here somewhere. I often see him. *C'mon!* Ol' man Crozier'll be home if we don't hurry."

Eddie caught up with Tom, but he kept thinking of the wonder of the woodpecker, his great body and red-crested head. I'll look him up when I get home, he thought, as they passed the old Bake and Brew House where Mr. Crozier now lived. The Bake and Brew House was one of the few remaining buildings on the Pennsbury Estate. Mr. Crozier had bought it and lived there alone, but he worked in Bristol, so was away all day. He didn't like it when the boys came to dig in the ruins, even though there was little to be found there except rusty hand-made nails, locks, hinges, and such things. He seemed to forget that he had been a boy once, himself. He shouted at them to "Get Out! Go home!" whenever he caught them there.

Pennsbury had been a beautiful mansion in William Penn's day, but it had been deserted for many years and had finally fallen into ruin. A great lead cistern on the roof, put there to collect rain water, had burst after freezing. The water seeped down into the timbers, rotting them so that the house collapsed. Over the years, things had been carried off till little remained but scattered bricks and rubble. Sometimes a bit of china could be found, and once Eddie had taken Ma a whole little plate which Ma said had been made in England and was a historic relic. She put it carefully away in the cupboard with other things Eddie had found.

Today, as the boys neared Mr. Crozier's house, they were very quiet, in case he might be home. They slipped through the trees near the river to the ruin, where they began searching as usual. Tom found a long, slender rattail hinge, but the part that had been on the doorframe was missing.

Eddie found only a rusty nail. Then he slipped down into the foundations to look around. There, he found a different kind of treasure that made him think of Ma. It made him think of Meg too. How she would love it! Under the steps that had led to the basement but now stood away from the foundation, covered with wet leaves, was a china doll's head. It wasn't even cracked! Eddie searched further through the leaves, and there was the leather body!

"Hey! Look what I've found!" he called to Tom. "A doll!"

"A *doll!* Who wants a *doll?*" said Tom disgustedly. "That's for *girls.*"

"It's for Meg. I told you she's no *girl;* she's a baby! Stop calling her a girl!" Eddie put the china head in his pocket and tucked the stained body inside his shirt.

But when Eddie showed the doll's head and body to Lavinia, she said, holding them close.

"Oh no, you mustn't give the doll to Meg. It's a historic relic and probably belonged to Letitia Penn, William Penn's daughter. Remember how Ma used to say we must always keep historic relics?"

Eddie nodded, "Yes," he said, "I remember. I guess even this old square-headed nail is a relic."

Lavinia, holding the doll's body, looked lovingly at the head. "I'll put it back together again," she said and took it with her to the kitchen.

Eddie went to the secretary to put away the nail among the great keys, door hinges, hasps, and other things. There was a little china pitcher too that Ma had loved. It had been found at Mount Vernon with a broken handle. Someone had mended it with a silver one so it looked very pretty. Ma thought it had belonged to Martha Washington. There too, was the engine Pa had made. Eddie took it down to look at it again. How did Pa ever do it? Eddie ran his fingers over the fascinating parts, the smokestack, the tiny whistle, the wheels. At every turn, the little bell tinkled. Just then, Pa came in and hung his hat by the door.

"Hello, boy!" he called, putting his hand on Eddie's curls. "I see you're interested in my locomotive again." Eddie looked up and smiled.

"Something wonderful about locomotives and trains," said Eddie, nodding.

"Yes, yes, wonderful! I'll never forget the time

I took you with me to Bridgeport. A freight train stood there on the siding and you said, almost in a whisper, 'Can I *touch* it?' Remember?" Eddie smiled again, recalling the time. "I was only four years old then, and I still feel that way," he said. "Something magic about trains."

"I hear Vinny in the kitchen, and something smells good. I guess supper is about ready." As Pa started toward the kitchen, Lavinia came in with the plates, stopping a moment to greet Pa.

"Supper's ready," she said. "Sit down. Eddie, did you wash?" Eddie vanished. He always forgot until Vinny reminded him.

As they all sat down, Pa spoke of the model engine again.

"I took a lot of pains with that model. I began it after the first run I made from Philadelphia to Morrisville. It was the Baldwin 4-2-0. I knew every lever and linchpin on her, and I can hear that whistle now."

Eddie knew what 4-2-0 meant. Pa had explained that long ago. It means four pilot wheels, two big driving wheels, and no wheels behind the drivers.

As Pa served, Eddie asked, "Pa, what's a

linchpin?" He had kept the model near him on the table, hoping Pa would go on and tell one of his famous stories about the railroads.

"A linchpin," Pa said, pleased that Eddie was so interested, "is a small rod through the center of the axle to hold the wheel in place. See?" Pa picked up the little engine and pointed it out. He went on musingly, "I remember how as a boy I was interested in mechanical things. Then, when I was older, I used to go to Bordentown to a shop where there were all kinds of fascinating things going on and where I picked up a good deal of information. The men in charge were good enough to let me watch whatever they were doing. They explained as they went, so I learned a great deal. Later, I was employed as a mechanic there in the Camden-Amboy Company. Yes, the very company I work for now. There was a young man there who was assembling a British-built locomotive called the John Bull. He had a funny name—Isaac Dripps." Pa chuckled. "But in spite of that, he became famous for his unusual ability, especially in building locomotives."

"Dripps!" said Eddie, laughing. "He *Dripps!*" But he leaned toward Pa to hear more.

"That company had an engine in service as early as 1833. That engine made quite a stir! And I piloted her on the Tamaqua and Schuylkill Railroad. It was my first job as an engineer. She was called the *Catawissa* and she looked like this." Pa sketched the little engine, saying, "She was the third locomotive to run in Pennsylvania."

As Pa finished his supper, folded his napkin, and rose from the table, Vinny said, "Did you see what Eddie found in the ruin today?"

"Oh, yes, I forgot," said Eddie. "Where did you put it, Vinny?"

"On the kitchen table. I put the head and the body back together again."

Pa was interested in the doll and agreed that it had surely belonged to Letitia Penn and must be

CATAWISSA

preserved. Lavinia put it on the shelf with the other treasures, and Eddie took up the engine to put it away.

"Some day," he said, "perhaps *I* can make a model engine too."

"Why not?" said Pa. "You can study each part and draw it to scale before you begin. That would help you in making it. Meantime, you can collect bits of this and that. Think about it! Now *there* is where your drawing will come in handy."

But drawing was not all that Eddie was interested in. He was good at fixing things, such as putting new washers in the pump, mending a leak in the hen-house roof, setting a register in the floor of Vinny's bedroom so the heat from the kitchen stove would not be lost. When Vinny's ring fell down the register, Eddie took it apart and found it for her.

"Oh, I'm so glad to have it back!" Vinny said, thanking him. "Ma gave it to me when I was six. You really are smart."

2 *Think* about it? Yes, Eddie thought, I *will* think about building a model engine. He remembered the day Pa had taken him to Bridgeport and how excited he had been. Pa had been talking to the engineer and the brakeman while Eddie stood in awe at the steaming engine that seemed almost alive. He wanted to touch it as if to be a part of such a wonder. The smokestack was of a different shape from the model Pa had made. Pa said the model was the *Black Hawk,* built in Philadelphia by the Bald-

win Company. Remembering, he thought, Maybe I'll make that one I saw at Trenton. I'll ask Pa about it.

From then on, Eddie began collecting bits of metal that might be of use in making a model engine. He searched the drawer in the kitchen table where there was a boxful of odds and ends— screws, small nails, a piece of hollow metal flared at the top. Ah-h-h! The very thing! It would do for the smokestack! Eddie pocketed the little treasure, and all day it was a reminder of the model engine he would make, and provided a secret excitement. I'll keep things in that little shell box Grandpa brought me from the seashore.

Summer had really arrived with hot, sunny days that brought the flowers out in Ma's garden. It brought weeds too, and now, it fell to Eddie to do the weeding. Ma had always done it. She said she loved the feel of the earth. Vinny was busy house cleaning. Weeding was not Eddie's favorite pastime. "But it *has* to be done!" Vinny said. "And be sure you don't pull up plants! And don't forget to edge the bed!" Vinny sounded like a grown-up woman.

Still, when it was done, the whole yard looked

better. Especially when the grass is cut, thought Eddie.

Sometimes Tom helped, then they went swimming off the Quinton dock. What fun it was! Tom's red hair and freckles stood out against his white skin, and Eddie's curly hair just wouldn't smooth down when it was wet, but curled more than ever. Tom had his own chores to do, grass to cut, trash to burn, and often had to help his father with his fish business. Mr. Devlin had a small shop where he sold the fish he caught in the Delaware—bass, crappies, and there were *always* sunfish. In the spring, there were shoals of shad to be caught. Tom and Eddie often went with Mr. Devlin or, if the skiff was free, they went by themselves or, if the tide was high, they fished from the dock. When it rained, Eddie had his drawing to interest him, but Tom had no liking for it. One rainy day, Tom came up from where he lived to see if Eddie had any idea of something to do. He dripped water on Vinnie's kitchen floor from his wet rubber coat, but Vinny just wiped it up and said, "Never mind. It's all right. Eddie brought in rain too. He's reading upstairs. Why don't you go up?"

Tom found Eddie stretched out on the floor reading Cooper's *Last of the Mohicans*. The boys had read together the first few chapters.

"Hey!" he said excitedly. "Listen to this!" Tom settled himself on the floor too. Eddie went on " 'To cover! To cover!' cried Hawkeye, who had just then dispatched his enemy; 'to cover, for your lives! the work is but half ended!' " Eddie read the last paragraph, then said, "That's the end of the chapter. Hey! Let's play Indians! The rain has stopped, and I'll tell you about the part you haven't read."

They clattered down the back stairs, through the kitchen where Vinny was baking bread. "Ummm." The boys sniffed the delicious fragrance as they passed the oven. "When will it be done?" called Eddie as he went out the door.

"In about fifteen minutes," said Vinny. "But you'll have to wait till it cools a little."

The wet grass felt good on bare feet and even the dripping from the trees was welcome after the hot June weather as the boys ducked behind bushes, making believe they were Indians— Squanto and Chingachgook. They had dipped into the mud in the path and daubed themselves with "war paint," each looking fiercer than the other, laughing so uproariously that it was hard to make believe they were enemies.

The heat continued into July with high humidity. The boys spent a lot of time swimming. Then, one day, Eddie suggested a plan.

"Let's camp out—what do you say?" He stood with his hands on his hips, legs spread. "We've got that old tarpaulin Pa used to use to keep the wood dry."

"Great!" said Tom. "If Ma will let me."

"Of course, I have to ask Pa too," said Eddie. "There's a place right down there where that big oak stands. It's far enough away so we can be on our own, and it's close to the river. The bank kind of levels off there too. It seems just right, hunh?"

"Let's go and ask Ma right now," said Tom, "and you can ask your dad when he comes home."

Off they trudged along the river, not even stopping at Penn's Manor to hunt for treasure. Ma's answer was yes, after she had questioned the boys about where they would camp and what protection they would have. She gave them a sack of potatoes to bake, with a couple of eggs on top, and found an old thick blanket for Tom to sleep in.

"Mind, now," she said. "Hold the eggs safe, or you'll have a mess. And be careful about fire!"

"We will!" Tom hurried out after Eddie, for fear his mother might change her mind. Women were so scary.

When Pa came home, the boys had a great heap of stuff ready for staying out all night. They had already found the tarpaulin and had begged clothesline from Vinny, to attach it to the lower branches of the oak.

Pa nodded his head when he saw it from across the lawn. "I see you have made up your minds without asking me. Well, I was a boy once, too. I guess it's all right. Be careful where you build your fire, and be sure there are no twigs near, no leaves!"

Eddie promised to be careful. "Yes, Pa. We borrowed the tarp from the barn. It was up in the loft, remember?" Pa nodded.

"Yes, we used to put it over the woodpile, but now we keep the wood on the porch. It was easier for Ma there." Pa gazed off into the distance. Thinking of Ma, thought Eddie.

Vinny gave the boys a kettle of stew she had made and a loaf of her homemade bread. There was a bit of bacon left, so she added that and lent them the small iron skillet for cooking.

The boys hunted for forked sticks strong enough to hold a crossbar to hang the kettle on. "And look!" said Eddie, "I brought along that hook we found one day, remember?" He held the iron hook for a moment, lost in thought.

It was used this same way one hundred and fifty years ago. How had they cooked? How had they been dressed?

"Oh, yes," he said aloud. "They cooked in the fireplace in the big mansion."

"*Who* did? What are you talking about? You're dreaming again. Who cooked in the fireplace?"

Eddie laughed. "I guess I *was* dreaming. I just wondered how this hook might have been used a hundred and fifty years ago, that's all." He hung it on the green stick they had put in the crotched uprights. There were plenty of stones on which to build the fire, and, soon, they had the stew bubbling, sending out enticing odors of onion, carrot, and meat, spiced as Ma had taught Vinny.

The first night was as pleasant as anyone could ask. It was bright moonlight, the river swooshed gently against the bank, and the boys sat by the dying embers of the fire till they were too sleepy to sit up. Eddie scattered the ashes, Tom spread out the blankets, and, with scarcely a word said, they were asleep.

Breakfast was not so easy as they had thought. The bacon half-cooked, the eggs too hard. But Vinny's bread was as good as always. The morning was bright and hot, so after the boys washed their plates in the river and scrubbed the pan with sand, they slipped in and had a swim. Eddie climbed up the bank and ran to the tree, with Tom after him.

"I'll beat ya to the top," he cried, catching up. But Eddie was first, after all. They had to scramble past clinging vines, scratching legs and arms, but when they reached the topmost branch, the view was glorious.

"I can see all over Jersey!" Eddie exclaimed; "and 'way down almost to Philadelphia!"

"I can too! I can see a big ship 'way down the Delaware," Tom cried, as he clung to the branch nearby. "It's like being in heaven!" he said.

Eddie, who was a little higher, said, "I see Mr. Crozier's house and the ruin and everything. And the old river just goes on and on. Oh yes, I see the ship too." 1962353

"I can't hold on any longer," said Tom sliding down from branch to branch.

"Me neither." Eddie followed. As they neared the ground, Eddie discovered that the vines held ripening grapes, tart and delicious.

Tom had to prove himself by hanging by his feet to pick them.

"They taste better this way," he said.

What a long, lazy day it was—in and out of the water swimming, lying on the bank in the sun, eating wild grapes, cooking fish they had caught.

"We have to tidy up the camp," said Eddie, taking his plate to wash it in the river. They had eaten the last of Vinnie's stew, and there was the pot to wash too.

After they had scattered the ashes, they lay on the bank a while, lazily watching the occasional passing skiff and the oncoming ship, happily tired.

When the sun had set and darkness crept over the river, Eddie yawned. "I'm sleepy," he said. "I'm going to turn in."

"Me too," agreed Tom.

They rolled up in their blankets and in minutes were asleep. Soon after they had gone to sleep, it began to rain harder and harder until it became a downpour. Eddie woke up first. He was chilled and at first didn't know where he was. Then he shouted:

"Hey! Wake up Tom! We're swamped!" He shook Tom's shoulder.

"Wha'—whassa matter?" But even as he spoke, the water touched his toes. With very few words, they hastily gathered up blankets, caps, and jackets. They left what little food there was, and the tarpaulin, and slogged through the woods that edged the bank.

Eddie's teeth chattered as they raced through the rain in the early dawn light toward Eddie's house.

Pa came in his night shirt to let them in. He laughed when he saw them.

"Two drowned rats!" he said. "Come in to the stove and get warm. I'll throw down some dry clothes for you." Pa went up the back stairs, and the boys took off their sodden clothes. As they dressed, Eddie started to giggle. "We were such wonderful campers," he said, and that started Tom. It became one of those times when the least move, the slightest word sets off gales of laughter. Each time one looked at the other, they were off again, till Vinny came down, dressed for the day.

"*What are* you two laughing at?" That started them off again, and they were still at it when Pa came down ready for work.

"Now stop it, you two, you've become hysterical. You, Eddie, go in the other room till you can control yourself." Eddie went obediently choking down his laughter. As he went through the doorway, he knocked lightly on the door frame, and Tom was off again. Pa spoke sternly, "Stop!" he said, and Tom did.

3 It was nearing the end of summer.
Dame school would begin soon. Eddie
and Tom spent the day roaming along the river
front, ending up at the old ruin as they so often
did. Tom found a rattail latch of a different
shape from the one he had found before, but
Eddie couldn't find anything. He was just about
to give up and go home, when his fingers touched
metal. It was a buckle, black with age and expo-
sure. It didn't look like much of a find, but as he

turned it about, a slight gleam on one edge made him think it might be worth keeping. He showed it to Tom,

"Yes," Tom agreed. "It might be worth showing your dad." Eddie nodded and slipped it into his pocket. "I'll see what Pa says."

"Let's go," said Tom. "I'm hungry. See you tomorrow." The boys went their separate ways.

What would Vinny have for supper? Eddie was suddenly hungry too. There was a chill in the air reminding him of fall. He thought of Ma and wished she could be there when he reached home. Pa had just arrived, and he had news to tell.

"Well, youngsters, what do you think? The officers of the Pennsylvania Railroad want me to take the first full run from Philadelphia to Pittsburgh. What do you think of *that?*"

"Oh, you must be the best engineer in the country," said Lavinia, hugging Pa.

"It's great! Simply great!" Eddie took Pa's hand in his own.

"I'm afraid it means that we'll have to move to Pittsburgh," said Pa. "That will be my headquarters. Vinny, you will stay in the East and go to that boarding school where you wanted to go. You can

spend the weekends at Grandma's here and come
with us during the summer. How's that?"

"Oh, I'd love it!" Vinny exclaimed, throwing
her arms around Pa's neck. "Then I can be with
my friends from Dame school. I'll miss you and
Eddie, though."

"Well, it's quite an honor for me, I must say."
Pa sat down, smiling, as he said musingly, "I
mind the year I went with the Tamaqua and
Schuylkill Railroad as engineer. How proud I

was! The new road had just opened and we hauled coal from the mines to the canals. You know, the railroad had been developed mainly to support the canals, and *I* drove the first engine to go over it.

"Of course, in those days, there was no cab on the engine. It had been built in Enland where I guess they don't mind the rain and the snow!" Pa laughed. "But having no cab had its advantages. There was a grand view of the mountains from the driving platform and, in case the train left the track, which it sometimes did, it was easier to jump free."

"Mountains?" queried Eddie, "Are there *mountains?*" He leaned close to Pa, and Vinny was just as close on the other side. They didn't want to miss a word.

"Mountains—yes, the Alleghenies. They stretch for a good many miles. Then there is Blue Mountain and Tuscarora we must cross, but I believe there is a stationary engine to haul the train up the incline and ease it down the other side. You know trains have been running on the Main Line of the Pennsy for twenty years, but only as far as Columbia. The Juniata River runs along there and the Main Line follows it for quite a way. Nice view there. From there, freight has been going on to Pittsburgh but transferring at Columbia to canalboat. It's pretty exciting to know that now trains will go all the way by steel rail to Pittsburgh. Of course, it's a pretty long trip. It will take three days and two nights. *Think* of it!"

"And *you* are the engineer!" exclaimed Eddie. "Whee!" He took a few turns around on his heel. Pa laughed. He was excited too. Vinny hugged herself to keep the shivers down.

"There will be difficulties at first, of course, but I expect we'll be able to overcome them. There will be woodpiles and water tanks along the way to keep the engine fed. I have a rough map to show where to look for them. And there will be whistle stops for the convenience of passengers who live in small communities. Wait till you see it."

The thought of seeing it brought back all the excitement and wonder Eddie had felt on seeing his first train. It had seemed almost alive, that engine, with its puffing and steaming. Then a sad thought came to him. What would he do without

Tom? Without Grandpa and Grandma, Aunt Ellen and Uncle Steve?

Eddie suddenly remembered the buckle he had been juggling back and forth in his hands. He showed it to Pa, who said,

"Oh. Where did you find this? Down there at Penn's Manor?"

"Yes, Pa, just when we gave up finding anything. Is it worth keeping?"

Pa had been rubbing it between his fingers. "Yes," he said, "I should think it is quite well worth keeping. It is a silver shoe buckle, probably once on Letitia Penn's shoe and, by the way it's made, the handwork of Francis Richardson. It is quite a treasure. We'll polish it and put it with the others. They must go into a special box, to take with us when we move."

"Let me take it, Pa," said Vinny. "I'll polish it." She took it to the kitchen and, in a few moments, brought it back, with its silver brightly shining.

Just then, Aunt Ellen came in the door to borrow some oil for the lamps.

"I just ran out," she said. "I meant to buy some at the market the other day, but I forgot it. I de-

clare, that child Meg makes me forget everything!" Aunt Ellen laughed shakily. "Did you
hear what she did today?"

Lavinia shook her head. "I thought once I
heard her scream, but I was cleaning in the back
parlor and when I didn't hear her again, I went
on working. What did she do?"

"She got out of my sight while I was scrubbing
the kitchen floor," Aunt Ellen went on. "She
went down the bank and fell into the river. I
heard a sort of scream and a gasp as she fell in,
but by the time I got to the door a passing boat
had rescued her. It took me quite a few minutes
to get down to the dock to pick her up and to
thank people for saving her. When I took her
from the man in the boat, she didn't want to
come with me! They must have made a good deal
of her in that few minutes. And listen to this!
When I had washed her and dressed her again,
and the boat was on its way back, she ran down
to the dock and jumped in! I guess she thought it
a great lark. What do you think of *that?*"

"I think something drastic ought to be done
about that," said Pa. "I think she should be pad-
dled." He got up to fill Aunt Ellen's oilcan.

"She was," said Aunt Ellen. "And now I've got a rope around her waist with a flat iron on the other end. But when the sun gets hot, she picks up the flat iron and goes into the shade. It doesn't seem to occur to her that she could carry it with her and run away!" They all laughed.

Yes, thought Eddie, as Aunt Ellen left, I'll miss Meg too. I wonder where we will live? Where

Meg

will I go to school? I'll miss my teacher; she was always so good to me when I didn't know my sums, especially since Ma was gone. All at once, the excitement changed to sadness. I'll miss Vinny, too, he thought, and I will miss the river. Where will I find a friend like Tom? And there will be no place to hunt treasure. I guess I don't want to go. Still, it will be wonderful to see that engine. "Oh yes, Pa says there are mountains!" he said out loud. Vinny looked startled. "Yes, mountains," she said. "What made you say that all of a sudden—daydreaming?"

"I guess so," Eddie said. "I was just remembering all the things I would miss if we move to Pittsburgh."

"I'll miss you too, but Pa says I can come to Pittsburgh on vacations, and maybe by summer we can have our own house there. There will be lots to see on the way. Pa says there are Indians living near Altoona. *Indians!*"

"Indians? Is that true, Pa?"

Pa was busy looking through the coat closet to see what could be left behind. There were outgrown coats and shabby ones and odds and ends

47

of things on the shelf. "Oh yes. I've seen them once or twice. They have a camp not far from the town. Senecas, I believe, from New York State. They keep going farther and farther west, but the country is fast building up and changing their way of life. It's a pity." He went on sorting things. "Do you still want this coat?" he called out to Vinny.

"Where will we sleep, Pa?"

"Oh, there are places along the way. Boardinghouses and small hotels have sprung up to accommodate the men who built the road and the stations as well as passengers and crewmen. They tell me there are plenty of places for meals and rest stops." By now, Pa had quite a heap of things to dispose of. Vinny had cleared away the supper things, and as she was putting dishes into the cupboard, the Quintons came in. Grandpa had told them the news and that the moving would take place in a few days.

"Might just as well do something to help," said Aunt Ellen. "Let's begin with those dishes. Do you still have that old sugar barrel?"

"Yes, in the barn. We'll have to get sawdust

from the mill to pack up the dishes." Pa lifted the heap of discarded clothing. "Here," he said, "these can go to the mission, Grandma."

"They will be welcome, I'm sure," Grandma said, making a bundle of them and putting them by the door.

Eddie followed as Grandpa went with Pa to the barn to collect the tools he kept in the shed—awls and hammers, saws and chisels. Most of them were already in place in the toolbox, but there were also several sheets of copper and brass and boxes of screws and nails.

A-ah, thought Eddie, there will be things I can use to build my engine! It was a good chance for Pa and Grandpa to talk. They had the same interest in railroads, and both had moved from place to place as their work made it necessary.

"We shall miss you," Grandpa said, as they tied up the box of tools. "But some day, we'll get together. Vinny will come to see us, and some day you will have a house where we can visit you. I suppose you will stay with Sally for now."

Pa and Grandpa joined the others on the porch in the waning summer light. Eddie sat on the step, thinking how pleasant it was. Would Pittsburgh be as pleasant? Would he like Aunt Sally?

That was a busy week. Aunt Ellen gave every spare moment to helping Vinny. The weather held fair so that Meg could be outdoors, tethered to the flat iron. Tom and Eddie helped as much as they could, fetching and carrying. A certain shyness kept them from discussing their separation.

Pa had arranged with a farmer to take Nellie and the chickens. When he drove off with Nellie tied to the end of his wagon, Eddie went into the barn and up into the hayloft where he stayed for some time, alone. Tom helped Pa clean out the stall.

By the end of the week, while Vinny was still washing up the last of the dishes and putting them into the barrel, a large moving van came, drawn by two great shire horses. Pa nailed on the lid of the barrel. Two men loaded the boxes and barrels. They took the chairs and other furniture and, by noon, the house was empty. It was no longer home. It was a haunting memory, echoing as they walked out on the bare boards.

Good-bys were said, again and again, with a
few tears. Pa and Eddie rode with the driver of
the van the twenty-five miles to Philadelphia.
The other man rode inside with the furniture.

Pa and the driver had a good deal to talk about,
and Eddie had his beloved river to watch all the
way.

4 It was well into the afternoon when they reached the marshaling yard, where freight cars stood to be loaded and the brand-new passenger car was in position to be coupled to the train. Eddie couldn't wait to touch its shiny newness, to go inside and see how it looked.

Pa and the driver of the van went on to unload the furniture into the freight car, and Pa said, "Don't be long, son; we've got a new engine to see!"

"Yes, Pa, I'll be right there! I've just *got* to see this new car."

Eddie's hand stroked the smooth paint, then he went up the steps and peeked in the door. He didn't quite dare go inside. There was the unloading of the furniture to see and the new freight car! Eddie flew down the steps and ran to where Pa had just stepped down from the van. Eddie looked into the empty car. The men were just beginning to unload the van.

"Just in time!" said Pa. "You and I have an appointment with a new engine." Eddie skipped along beside Pa as they went from the marshaling yard to the roundhouse. It was impossible to simply walk! Pa laughed.

"I think I am almost as excited as you are," he said. "And there it is!" And there it was! Its great smokestack sending out a lazy mist of smoke, just waiting for its first run. What a beauty she was! Her name was painted on the side, the F. K. HEISLEY. Everything seemed to shine—the bell, the whistle, the steel driving rods. There was fancy ironwork supporting the huge headlight and the cowcatcher was of a new design.

And the smokestack! It seemed to be as high as a house. It, too, was different in design from those that had been built before.

"Look, son," Pa said, taking Eddie's arm. "Remember the story I told you about the 'grasshopper run'? Well, this is a new device to keep it from happening again. See that box on the engine? That holds sand. When I push a certain lever, sand is released into this tube which leads right down to the track to give traction."

Eddie nodded. He remembered the story. One late summer, a train near Lancaster had run into a swarm of locusts. They had been crushed under the wheels, making the track so slippery the train wouldn't move. Now, with the sandbox, this would not happen again.

The engine stood in the roundhouse, ready to go onto the turntable, then from there to the track leading to the station. Two men operated the switch with levers, one at each end of the movable track. It seemed like magic to Eddie that the great "iron horse" could be moved by men using levers. In moments it stood on the new track, ready to go. Pa climbed into the engine cab, Eddie standing ready to follow if Pa seemed willing. At first, Pa was occupied with the new levers and handles, the cords and chains leading to whistle and bell to brake and throttle. Then he turned and called, "Come aboard, son," and Eddie was beside Pa in seconds, grinning from ear to ear.

"You can ride here with me to the station, boy, but after that, you must ride in the coach, at least for a while until I am used to the old girl and her gadgets. Now, we must pick up the coach and freight car standing over there."

Pa opened the throttle and moved the engine forward while a brakeman turned a switch. Then Pa backed to the freight where the brakeman coupled the two cars, freight and passenger, to the engine. When the brakeman blew his whistle, they continued backing into the station, which was not far away, and into the dark shed.

The conductor, who was aboard the passenger car, came out to greet Pa, and there, awaiting the new arrival, were several officials of the Pennsylvania Railroad. Pa seemed to know them all, and Eddie guessed that Pa had been chosen to run the train by the consent of all because he was the best engineer in the whole world. When the men had all shaken hands with Pa, they turned to Eddie.

"What do you think of this father of yours, young man? Isn't he great?"

Eddie bowed, as Ma had taught him, and said, "Yes, sir. How do you do, sir?"

Then one of the others said, "We are all having supper at Green's Hotel and expect you to join us in a kind of celebration. Is it all right with you, Mr. Moore?"

"Of course, of course," Pa said. "We expect to spend the night there, don't we, son?" Eddie felt as if he were one of the men, they made him so welcome.

The supper in honor of Pa and the opening of the new road to Pittsburgh was very grand, and a complete new experience for Eddie.

"It's the very first time I've stayed in a hotel," he said to Pa, as they went to their room to leave their things.

"Yes," said Pa, "but we just do everything as we always have done. You know the right way, as Ma and I have taught you. Just be yourself." Pa smoothed Eddie's hair as he so often did. Somehow, the gesture helped Eddie to feel comfortable at the table, to enjoy listening to the talk among the men as they discussed the new engine and its special features. It was rather past Eddie's usual bedtime when the men left, but excitement kept him awake till they had gone. Then Pa said,

"Tomorrow is a big day! Let's get to bed." And, surprisingly, Eddie fell asleep almost as soon as his head hit the pillow. In the morning, Pa woke him gently.

"Come, boy," he said, "this is it!"

While they ate breakfast, Pa told about his first stay in a hotel.

"Here we are! Here in Philadelphia! Let's make the most of it. I recollect *my* first stay in a hotel. It was in Portsmouth. I had just been made engineer with the Portsmouth and Roanoke Railroad and was to take charge of the engine in the morning. I was so excited I could hardly eat the dinner they set before me, and I slept very little. Of course, I had been studying engineering, but had not yet run a train. The engine was the *John Barnett*. What a thrill that was!"

"Was it scary when you really drove your first engine?" asked Eddie, thinking of the shiny *F. K. Heisley* and its enormous smokestack.

"I don't know as you would say scary exactly. There were many things to keep track of and to watch because of its being more powerful than any engine before that. We had to go steadily so as not to derail the train, my hand on the throttle all the way, bells to ring, the whistle at crossings, see that the fireman kept the steam up; oh, lots of things. It was very satisfying when all went well. Sometimes, it didn't."

Eddie could just imagine what it had been like. How he hoped Pa would let him ride in the cab and *maybe* blow the whistle for the crossings. He wondered if any other boy had so wonderful a father as he.

"Those men must think you are the best engineer in the country when they have you make that first run from Philadelphia to Pittsburgh, on the Main Line!" Eddie said proudly.

"Oh, I don't know," Pa said, laughing. "Maybe they all saw that piece in the paper about the stationary engine I built before I was twenty-one. Did I tell you about it?"

"No, sir, tell me," said Eddie.

"Well, I guess I have a feeling for mechanics, just as you have. We all have some special quality, I believe, but it must be developed. I was pretty happy when they wrote that piece about my engine. I recollect a part of it. It went something like this: 'A steam engine of peculiar construction, which occupies a surprisingly small space and works with admirable and speedy precision. The inventor and constructor, Edward Terhorst Moore, is entitled to great praise since he is not yet twenty-one.' Well, my father said, when he read it, 'You can do anything you *really* want to do.' And I believe you can."

Eddie decided he believed it, too.

"Come, son, it's time to pack our things and go. This is the big day!"

They walked down Market Street to the station at Sixth, with Eddie looking in store windows on the way and wondering at all the strange people in the city. No one seemed to know anyone else. Would Pittsburgh be like that? Would he find friends?

As it had been the day before, officials were standing by the engine examining all the new features, the sandbox, the improved engine cab with a little corner place for the fireman to stand and a toolbox where he could sit. On the other side was a small folding seat for the engineer. One of the men saw Eddie's eager look and boosted him into the cab.

"I know how you feel, son. Go on have a real look!" he said.

There hadn't been time in that short run from the marshaling yard for Pa to explain everything. Now, he pointed out the throttle which controlled the amount of steam for the engine, the speed, fast or slow, stopping and starting. A cord led to the whistle, another to the bell. Pa opened the firebox to show Eddie how the steam pipes were heated, then the water gauge controlling the flow of water to make steam. Eddie was so excited his stomach felt funny. At the same time, he felt as if his feet scarcely touched the floor. Very strange! The fireman who stood close by, laughed, clapping Eddie on the back.

"She's some ol' girl, this engine—right?"

"Oh-oh-o-o! *Great!*" said Eddie as Pa eased him down the steps.

"We've got a run to make, remember?" Pa followed, joining the men of the crew and the others. The president of the railroad drew Pa forward and said, "Mr. Moore, I want you to meet our mayor of Philadelphia, Mr. Charles Gilpin."

They shook hands, then Pa said, "And this is my son, Edward, Mr. Mayor."

Eddie thought the excitement would never end. The mayor of Philadelphia!

Then, Pa said, "Isn't it time we got started?" He looked at his watch.

By this time, a few more passengers had gathered and, one by one had gone into the car. There were even a few women. It was time to be off.

Pa climbed into the cab of the engine, and Eddie went with the others into the passenger car. The brakeman took his place, the conductor blew the whistle and called *"All aboard!"*

Pa answered with two short toots, and the wheels turned slowly, gathering speed as they drew out of the station. Eddie sat close to the window where he could see everything. He had never been in Philadelphia before and had never seen houses strung together as they were, not far from the tracks. The houses all alike and built of brick. How did anyone know his own

house? How different from home! **HOME?** Where was home? Suddenly, Eddie felt very much alone.

As they left the center of the city, the houses were more scattered, though still in rows. In about twenty minutes, the land seemed to drop away so the roadbed was quite high above the street level. Pa rang the bell to warn people off the tracks as they approached the station where it said, HESTONVILLE. Pa whistled for the crossing. People crowded around the train, even standing on the tracks to see the new engine.

Most of them were happy and excited, but one man shook his fist angrily. "Invention of the devil!" he cried.

Not far off, to the right, Eddie could see a great park, green and lovely. The man sitting next to him saw his interest and said, "That's Fairmount Park, the largest park in the world!"

Then the conductor blew his whistle, Pa rang the bell, and they were on their way again. There was a confusion of voices as the passengers talked, but the only time Eddie paid any attention to what was being said was when he heard "Edward Moore." It seemed that everybody knew Pa's name!

There were several stops, the White Hall Hotel and Villanova, as they rode through the beauty of the Pennsylvania countryside, Eddie getting more and more hungry by the minute. Finally, Pa slowed down, then rang the bell and stopped at Paoli.

Again, there were crowds of people waiting. Young girls and boys danced up and down, a dog ran off, terrified, his tail between his legs, and an old man shouted "What about the cattle ye'll kill off, eh? What about *them?*" He, too, shook his fist at the puffing monster. Pa only smiled at him, as he waited for Eddie to reach him through the crowd.

"This is a rest stop, son, so we'll have a few minutes to get something to eat. I guess you can handle that, eh? How was it? Was it fun?" Pa took Eddie's arm and helped him through the crowd and into the lunchroom of the hotel.

"Nothing *like* it!" Eddie said as they slid onto stools at the counter.

"Remember," said Pa, "we must leave the instant we hear the conductor's whistle." They were served promptly, but so many people spoke to Pa, he hardly had time to eat. Suddenly, the whistle sounded. Pa rose, pulled Eddie off the stool while he still had part of his sandwich in his hand.

"See what I mean, son? When the whistle sounds, we *go!*" Then, with a wave of his hand, Pa left Eddie and went toward the engine. Two more passengers came aboard at Paoli. They looked as excited and happy as he was.

5   The Pennsylvania countryside was beautiful in its changing colors of early autumn. Where there were open fields, the earth was rich brown, plowed in even rows. Some were squares of green winter wheat and rye. He thought of Grandma's quilt, it was so neat and even, and of the Sunday school lesson about the "Promised Land."

About noon, they came to Downingtown where everyone got off the train for lunch. Pa was waiting for him.

"Now, son, don't forget what I told you. Choose what you want to eat as soon as you can, and be ready to leave when the whistle blows."

The lunch counter was round and in the center was a Lazy Susan, kept turning by a man who sat in the corner. The food was all set in the center, and as it turned, each person chose the dish he wanted. Eddie reached for a dish of macaroni and cheese and was about to take a pink dessert, but he was too late. It passed him by. Oh, well, he thought, I'll get it when it comes around again. Pa took a glass of milk for him and a roll from a basket. As Eddie gulped the last of the milk, he saw the pink dessert coming. Just then the whistle blew. Pa grasped Eddie's hand and pulled him off the stool. Too late! The pink dessert went sailing by.

"Too bad!" said Pa. "Next time, think fast. You're one of us men now, remember?" Pa boosted Eddie up into the passenger car. Eddie felt cheated, but he didn't say a word. "See you later," Pa said. Eddie didn't dare say how much he wanted to be in the engine cab.

It happened that one of the older men of the company came and sat beside Eddie. He was

older than Pa, maybe as old as Grandfather. He
smiled at Eddie and said, "This is quite an ad-
venture, eh? I'm Jerry Thomas, one of the
officials of the railroad."

"Oh yes, sir," Eddie said. "It's great!" And he
couldn't help adding, "You know it's my father
who is driving the engine."

"Yes, I know." Mr. Thomas smiled and nodded.
"We chose him because he is one of the best in
this country, we think."

The wheels were turning slowly, gradually increasing speed till the chuff-chuff, chuff-chuff, chuff became one long pu-urrrr of sound. Mr. Thomas went on talking. "While this road was a-building, we had many meetings to plan out the route, to decide on the scheduled stops, to arrange for men to lay the tracks, to decide who should be the crew and who the engineer. We all agreed—the engineer should be your father."

Edward grinned. He didn't know quite what to say in acceptance of such a compliment to Pa. Then, he said,

"We're going to live in Pittsburgh now—with my Aunt Sally. Pa says it will take us three days and two nights to get there; will it?"

"Yes, that's about it. Railroads are very new here, even yet. Many of those we hired to do the roadwork came from England. I mind how my father used to tell of the very first rails used there. It was in the time of Queen Elizabeth. The rails were laid for the horse-drawn carts that hauled coal and stones from the mines to the barges, then by water to different ports."

"Queen *Elizabeth?* Why that's hundreds of years ago!"

"Yes, rails were of wood then and soon wore out. Now, we have the very latest thing, steel rails, and a sandbox to give the wheels good traction. My grandfather, who lived in England, used to tell that when he was a boy they laid rails in certain streets in London for the horse-drawn coaches. It was more comfortable than riding over the cobbles. I guess you could call that the *first* railroad." Mr. Thomas yawned and stopped talking. Eddie wished he would go on. It was as good as hearing Pa tell about old times. Suddenly, the man's head drooped, his eyes closed and he was asleep.

How different he looks, thought Eddie, with his head falling aside. I wish I could draw him like that. Out came Eddie's notebook and pencil. Lightly and swiftly he caught the likeness, sketchy, but unmistakable. He had just tucked the pad away when Mr. Thomas snorted and woke himself.

"Well," he said, "I seem to have fallen asleep. Where are we?"

"We're just beyond Coatesville, sir," said Eddie, proud that he remembered.

In two minutes, Mr. Thomas was asleep again. Eddie gazed out of the window. It sometimes seemed as if the landscape moved and swept past the window, instead of the train moving.

As they went farther west, beyond Coatesville, it was more hilly and the train slowed going up the inclines. Sometimes there were long stretches of forest, and, once, Eddie saw a deer bounding off through the woods. He thought of Tom and the deer they sometimes saw near Penn's Manor. What was Tom doing? Where was he?

Mr. Thomas slept on.

As they neared Lancaster, Eddie heard the conductor speak to a man in the seat behind him. He said,

"This is a whistle stop, you know, sir. Who are you going to see?"

"I'm visiting the Ryans," the man answered.

"Oh, the Ryans. In that case, we can stop a half mile this side of the station. Their house is right near the tracks."

"Oh, thank you. That will be a help."

A road ran along the tracks, and a horse and buggy passed. A man and two children were in the buggy. The man had on a broad hat, his hair was rather long, and he wore a high collar instead of a white collar and tie, such as Pa wore. He looked like a preacher, thought Eddie. The children, too, were dressed differently from the way Eddie had always seen children. The little girl had a scoop bonnet and a large apron over her dress. The little boy wore a big hat like his father's. Then, they were gone.

Soon Eddie heard Pa blow the whistle for the crossing and they were pulling into Lancaster. There were many people, among the others, dressed as those he had seen passing the train.

Mr. Thomas was awake now, and, like Eddie, was looking out of the window. "Ah," he said, "Amishmen. Fine people!"

"What are Amishmen, sir?" asked Eddie.

"They are members of a religious sect who came to this country for religious freedom. They came from Germany about two hundred years ago and settled around here. I'm sure you noticed how beautifully they cultivate the land."

Mr. Thomas and Eddie moved toward the door, but kept talking.

"Oh yes, I noticed. But why do they dress like that, I wonder?"

"It is because they want to be separate from the world," Mr. Thomas answered. "Like the Mennonites, they 'dress plain' and live quiet lives." Eddie wasn't sure what he meant, but there was Pa waiting for him, and as always, men close to him talking about the engine. Still answering questions, Pa reached and pulled Eddie to his side. The people who had come to see the engine gradually thinned out.

The conductor and the brakeman were examining the underparts of the cars with a reflecting lantern, to make sure that all was well. Eddie stretched and turned to watch.

"That off-wheel there seems a little hot," he heard the brakeman say, "but I guess it's all right." "It isn't smoking," agreed the conductor. "I think it'll do."

"Well," said Pa briskly, "we must get on. We've lost five minutes already." He marched Eddie beside him into the lunchroom of the hotel.

"Don't forget, son," he said, laughing. "There's only time for a bite."

"I know," Eddie said, reaching for a glass of milk.

Almost before the milk was down, the conductor blew the whistle.

Pa waved to Eddie and climbed into the cab. Eddie looked after him for a moment then followed the passengers into the car. This time, Mr. Thomas sat with some of his friends, but greeted Eddie with a wave of his hand as he passed. How Eddie longed to be in the engine cab with Pa during a part of this historic journey. Pa *had* promised that perhaps after leaving Harrisburg he could ride with him for a while. He stared out of the window. The houses became more scattered, the beautiful fields giving way to the blue distance of hills. If only Ma had been with him to see it all!

As they ran through deep woods, Eddie saw the

flick of a tail of some animal vanishing in fear of the noise of the train.

Mr. Stewart, the conductor, came and sat down beside Eddie.

"How do you like being a passenger on this first run? It's quite a journey isn't it?"

Eddie nodded, "Yes, sir, it's wonderful. It seems as if the country stretched forever!" He didn't know quite how to express the feeling he had, excitement, wonder, homesickness, going he knew not where, not even knowing Aunt Sally.

Mr. Stewart seemed to understand.

"If you think this is wide and strange country, wait till you get to the mountains. I have been as far as Pittsburgh before, but then, we had to go by several stages, by train to Columbia, then by the Juniata River and canal, then on another railroad, the Portage, to Pittsburgh. It's quite a treat to know I can stay on this train all the way."

"Is Pittsburgh a nice city? Is it like Philadelphia?" Eddie wondered.

"Oh, no, it's not like Philadelphia at all. For one thing, it's hilly and nowhere near as old. There's a lot of industry there."

Seeing Eddie's puzzled look, he said, "I mean the manufacturing of various products, such as glass, steel, and so on. Most of the city is on this side of the Allegheny. Excuse me," he said, as Pa slowed down and rang the warning bell, then blew the whistle, "I must attend to business."

Eddie, watching from the window, saw the fireman gathering wood from a pile beside the track. Nearby, was a great water tank supported by a tall iron framework from which the fireman drew water to fill the engine. It took quite a while for refueling in preparation for the hills, so Eddie left the passenger car, as most of the men did, to look around. It was a chance to watch Pa as he examined the engine to make sure it was in running order. The conductor hung the blue lantern on the end of the train to warn any possible oncoming train not to couple on, and on the ground, he set a red lantern as well.

At last the crew took their places. Pa climbed into the engine calling to Eddie, "So long, son," and the passengers went back into the car. The men spoke kindly to him as he took his seat, and he overheard them speaking of Pa and how well everything was going.

Soon, they came to Columbia where two people left the train. By now those waiting at the station were carrying umbrellas, for it had begun to rain very hard. The tracks ran beside the Juniata, and as they went along, it seemed to rain harder and harder. Eddie could hear the men talking about it and saw them looking anxiously out of the window toward the river.

Eddie remembered the story his grandpa Quinton had told him. Once, when Grandpa was the engineer on the Camden and Amboy, the river had come right up and flooded the tracks. The rails and ties all floated away and the train had been stranded! Eddie hoped it wouldn't rain hard enough to make a flood now.

In a short time the train came into sunshine again. It had only been a shower. But what a story that was! He would have to remind Pa.

Mr. Stewart, the conductor, came back and sat down beside Edward.

"We had quite a shower, didn't we?" he said. "Being so near the river, I was a little anxious for a time for fear the track would be flooded."

Eddie nodded. "Yes, my grandfather once told me about when it happened."

"I've heard my father tell about that." Mr. Stewart nodded. "I know the story. Yes, I remember it. It will be interesting to see how we manage the Allegheny mountains. They tell me there are what they call 'inclines' and stationary engines with cables that will draw the train up the mountain. There will be several engines on the different inclines to then transfer the hook and cable to the rear of the train to ease it so it will go down slowly. I am anxious to see how well it works." Mr. Stewart got up and went to attend to his duties. They were slowing down for a small station, and Pa was ringing the bell. Then he blew the whistle for the crossing and stopped. HIGH SPIRE was on the small building near the tracks and Eddie could see a church not far away, with a tall steeple. The station was named for that, he thought. A man boarded the train, waving farewell to the people gathered to see the new engine. Mr. Stewart blew his whistle. The bell began ringing again and the chuff-chuff of alternating pistons began.

It was late afternoon. Eddie was tired and hungry. When would they be in Harrisburg?

6 Harrisburg? This is where Pa said they would eat dinner and stay the night and *maybe* tomorrow he could ride in the engine cab!

Mr. Stewart didn't come back to the seat for a while as he was talking to one of the officials farther back. Eddie wished he would come and tell more about his experiences with railroads.

After they had gone through many wooded hills that seemed to fold one into another, a few houses appeared, farms and barns, men harvesting in the fields. Horses and cattle thundered away from the noise of the train and chickens squawked and fluttered.

Finally, the farmland was behind them. Houses came closer and closer together, and they were in Harrisburg. Harrisburg! Where Pa had promised he might ride with him in the engine cab!

As the passengers left the train, one of the men put his arm around Eddie's shoulder and said,

"You have quite a father, boy. Do you know it?" Eddie just grinned and nodded. He couldn't speak.

The hotel was within easy distance of the station. There, they all went to freshen up, have dinner, and spend the night.

By now, Eddie was more used to eating in public places. Pa took him to a table in the dining room where several other men were sitting. They were all friendly, and Eddie listened eagerly to their conversation. They talked of the development of engines, the various kinds, but especially the changes in manufacture of locomotives and how the steam engine had brought in a whole new world.

When dinner was over and one by one the men left, Pa said,

"We must get to bed, son. I must be up early and go over the engine before we go on. Come."

Pa was not only able to operate a locomotive, he knew how to build or repair it. Besides his native ability, he had spent a great deal of time working in the Camden and Amboy shop. Eddie loved to watch him oil the joints of the driving rod, make sure the throttle worked smoothly, see that the steam valve operated correctly. He followed every move. Meanwhile, the fireman was on hand to stoke the fire, the brakeman checked the couplings between tender and coach and coach and freight cars. The passengers gathered to board the train, and Eddie noticed that there were new ones among them, one a woman. But this time, Eddie was to ride in the cab.

"You may ride in the cab with me as far as Lewistown. Then, we'll see. Perhaps you can stay with me as far as the next stop. That will be eighty-two miles. We'll see."

Edward knew that "we'll see" meant that if he was quiet and didn't get in Pa's way, he could stay. He squeezed back and sat on the tool chest back of where the fireman would stand.

"All ready?" Pa said to Mr. Murphy, the fireman, as he put on his gloves.

"All ready," agreed Mr. Murphy.

Pa pulled the bell rope, then the whistle cord, opened the throttle, and they ch-chu-chuffed out of the Harrisburg station.

It was pretty warm there by the boiler, but Eddie felt almost as if he too were driving that great engine.

At Rockville, they came to the long bridge over the Susquehanna. The sound changed and became a rumble and clatter. Pa said in a loud voice so Eddie could hear, "This is the new one and is only two years old! It is quite a wonder of construction. Look down!" Eddie had to twist his body to look as Pa pointed. He felt almost as if he were floating in air, it was so far down to where the river flowed. And it was so wide!

The noise of the engine made it impossible to talk to Pa. But Eddie knew that was out of the question anyway. Pa's eyes were glued to the road ahead, on the steam gauge, on the throttle, on the bell rope as they passed through settlements. His face was lighted up as the fireman opened the firebox door to put in more wood. Ed turned again to look out, but the space was cramped. It seemed very hot.

About midmorning, there was a rest stop. Everyone left the train and trooped to the tavern. As Pa helped Eddie down from the engine cab, he said, "Well, how was it? Pretty hot and a tight squeeze, eh?"

"Yes, it was hot, but it was great, Pa. Thank you. But I guess I'll sit in the coach for a while. But, honest, it was great! It was like going to the moon!" Pa chuckled.

"This next part of the journey will be interesting but somewhat difficult. The track winds in and out of the hills which are the beginning of the mountains. The train might even leave the track and that's bad, but we'll hope it won't."

The conductor blew the whistle for boarding, and Pa left him. Eddie took his seat near the front of the coach and the chuff-chuffing of the alternating pistons began. It was as Pa had said, the hills closed in at times so that Eddie felt as if they might stop the train altogether.

The sky was not as clear as it had been and as

the train gathered speed, it grew darker and darker and began to rain again. The tracks ran for miles along the Juniata, and as they went along, the rain came down in sheets. Eddie could hardly see beyond the window. He heard the men behind him talking about it and saw how they watched the river. It seemed to be rising.

"It may flood the tracks," said one.

"Yes, it looks rather bad," said another. Eddie couldn't help listening. What would Pa do if the track was flooded?

The first man said, "This reminds me of a time I've heard about. It was along the Delaware on the Camden and Amboy Railroad." Eddie pricked up his ears at the words "Camden and Amboy" and got up on his knees to face the man telling the story. The man winked at him and went on.

"As you know, only a year or two ago, warnings of trouble were carried by swift riders on horseback. Well, a frantic rider came down the line to warn the crewmen that it was dangerous for the train to continue its journey, for the Delaware was rising. There, too, the track was close to the river. However, the engineer thought he could get through safely even though the water did come over the rails, but it hadn't slowed the train, so he continued.

"As they went on, the water became deeper as the little train chuffed and snorted its way along. The ripples rose to swirls, the swirls to waves and —it stopped the train!" The man stopped a moment to clear his throat and looked to see how Eddie enjoyed the story, for Eddie was leaning forward ready at any moment to speak, but he kept still as the man went on.

"When the train stopped, the crew held a council, considering what to do. They decided to back up, and the engineer went into reverse. Suddenly, as true as I'm sitting here, the brakeman yelled 'Stop! Stop!' and blew his whistle for all he was worth. Then he shouted, *'The rails and cross-ties are floating!'*

"They could go neither forward nor back! The passing of the train had disturbed the weakened roadbed and they were stranded!"

Then Eddie spoke. "What do you think? My grandfather was that engineer!"

The man who had told the story looked surprised. Then he said, "Yes, by Jove! So he was!" Then went into a great laugh, slapping his knee.

"Well, to go on—Fortunately, there were farmers along the bank anxious about the fate of the train. One of them had a bright idea. "Come!" he called, beckoning as he went, "barn doors!" Eddie was as fascinated as if he had never heard the story. Would Pa get into such a fix? He wondered and looked out of the window. No, the track was not so near the river as it had been; the rain had slackened and they were safe. But the story went on—

"They levered the great doors off the hinges, launched them into the flood poling with fence rails to the stranded train and rescued the passengers and crew from the half-drowned train."

"What happened then?" questioned Eddie excitedly, as if he didn't know!

"The farmers and their wives made a holiday of it. They and the passengers all gathered at one house for a feast the women provided, then were taken to different farms for the night. The next day, the flood had subsided so a road crew could repair the tracks, and by the next day, they all went on their way."

What a story to tell Pa! That the men all knew about Grandfather's driving that train!

By now, they had run out of the rain; the sky cleared and the sun came out once more.

Mr. Stewart came back and sat down beside Eddie for a few minutes.

They were slowing down; Pa was ringing the warning bell. Mr. Stewart went to attend to his duties. Pa blew the whistle for the crossing and they stopped.

7 When it was time to go aboard again, Eddie decided that the passenger car was more comfortable than the engine cab, and he could see more from the window. He didn't have to tell Pa. Pa seemed to know. He said:

"I guess you've had enough of driving the engine, eh?" Eddie just grinned.

"Come, we shall be here only a few moments. Be sure to come quickly when the conductor blows the whistle." Pa looked at his watch, as he did so often to make sure they were on time.

Eddie watched as Mr. Stewart and the brakeman again looked under the freight and the passenger cars with the reflecting lantern. Pa joined them to see if there was anything wrong.

"That one box seems to heat up pretty badly," said the brakeman, "but it will cool while we stand here."

Pa went back to the engine to oil the valve gear, then went into the station office to see if there had been any telegraph messages about the road ahead. Eddie followed him. To think that only last year, in 1851, train dispatching was done by telegraph! But this trip was full of wonders.

The whistle sounded. Everyone took his place again on the train. Pa answered the whistle with two toots and again they were off.

Once more, Mr. Stewart sat beside Eddie. "I'm a little anxious about that hotbox," he said, "but we hope it will be all right. It seemed to cool down as we stopped."

The train had hardly picked up speed before Mr. Stewart suddenly jumped up, shouting to the brakeman, "Smoke and sparks!" running to the front of the coach, grabbing a red lantern as he went. He opened the front door, and went up the ladder to the top of the freight car, swinging the lantern and going as fast as he dared along the walkway to the engine. Already, Eddie felt the engine slow down, heard Pa ringing the bell. The fireman had seen the smoke, too.

Everyone was startled. Necks craned to look out of the windows, for by this time, smoke was pouring out from beneath the coach. Was it the hotbox? It was!

Suddenly, Pa reversed the engine near a water tower. Eddie followed the other passengers while the brakeman hung the blue lantern on to the end of the coach, to warn any oncoming train not to couple on, and a red lantern on the ground to warn of danger. Mr. Stewart came to get the reflecting lantern, but there was no need for that now. The hotbox was blazing. All the passengers tumbled out of the coach to see what had stopped the train and had gathered about the crew where the trouble was. Pa, too, came up just as Eddie joined them. Pa held his cap and scratched his head.

"Well, I guess this will hold us up for a while. The fireman saw the smoke and sparks came from that wheel we were concerned about, and in no time it was ablaze. 'Twill be well past noon before the box has cooled enough for the brakeman to renew the oiled packing and get the wheel in running order," said Pa. Meanwhile the passengers sat on fence rails, walked in the woods, or sat waiting in the coach.

Pa went about his own work, oiling the places on the engine that needed constant attention.

Eddie watched for a while, then walked toward the woods where the ground rose steeply. He started to climb the hill, then, thinking he had heard Pa call, he stopped to listen but heard only the talk and busyness of the people from the train. He reached the top of the hill and went deeper into the woods, where he could see horses tethered and beyond them still farther, teepees! Indians! He went on and on. Indians! He couldn't wait to tell Tom. Tom? Of course he *couldn't* tell Tom! Tom was miles and miles away!

Eddie stood in a small clearing at the far edge of the strip of woods. A woman was tending a pot hung from a bar held by crotched sticks just like he and Tom had built! Just then, a boy came from the other side of the teepee. He saw Eddie at once and for a moment stared at him, then came slowly toward him. Eddie stared back. They were like two puppies, each waiting for the other to make the first move. Then the Indian boy said, "Hi, me Seneca."

And Eddie answered, "Me Philadelphia, no—Pittsburgh!" Just then, the whistle blew! Eddie turned and ran as fast as he could, back through the woods, over broken branches and briers, caught by twigs, brushed by leaves.

He arrived at the train just as it had begun to move!

Luckily, Pa saw him and stopped. Eddie, all out of breath, climbed aboard and fell into a seat. What would Pa say? But he had seen *Indians*!

The man in the seat next to Eddie said, "Well! That was a close call! I thought perhaps you had gone with your dad into the engine. Where were you?"

"I went into the woods to see if there were any animals. Then I saw a teepee and horses, so I went on and I met an Indian boy! I didn't mean to go so far. Pa always told me to stay nearby so

I would hear the conductor whistle. But I forgot; it was so exciting!"

"I can imagine," the man said. "The Indians are going farther and farther west, and soon we shall never see them in this part of the country. Sad."

Eddie could see Mr. Stewart at the front of the coach. He seemed too busy to sit down. He was constantly on the lookout for danger, and much of the time stood on the back platform to watch with the brakeman for anything unusual, such as another hotbox or anything that might catch fire from the sparks of the engine. There were trees of the great forest so close to the track that sometimes it seemed as if the branches brushed the roof of the coach.

Eddie had never been so hungry. There were miles and miles without a single building where one could find food or rest.

Finally, after a long curve and a long gradual descent, they came to Altoona. There was the usual crowd to see the arrival of the train, and the passengers could hardly get down the steps for the press of people. The confusion of voices, each trying to be heard above the others, was deafening. Eddie couldn't find Pa and was carried along by the crowd into the station. At one side was a counter with food for sale. Eddie was so hungry he could hardly wait, but Pa finally came through the mass of people and greeted him.

When the whistle blew, and the conductor called "All-aboard!!" Pa took Eddie's hand and helped him to the coach through the mass of curiosity seekers and passengers. There were several new passengers to go aboard, one of them a girl about Eddie's age. He saw her father pay the conductor for her journey and, as he left and waved good-by, the girl began to cry. She sat just opposite Eddie and she cried and cried, her face in her hands. At last, he could stand it no longer. He remembered Vinny and how she had looked so sad when he and Pa had left. He reached over and touched her sleeve. "Hey," he said, "what's the matter? Where are you going?"

The girl lifted her head, still sobbing jerkily.

"To my grandmother's."

"Aren't you glad to be going to your *grandmother's?*" asked Eddie, puzzled.

"But my father sold me. He *sold* me! Didn't

you see how he gave the conductor money?" She covered her face again, wailing.

"But *that* was to pay your *fare,* don't you see?" The girl suddenly stopped crying and looked at Eddie in amazement.

"What? Pay my fare? Is *that all?*"

"Of course. Say, what's your name? Mine's Eddie. Eddie Moore. What's yours?"

"Chrissy," said the girl, "Chrissy Wallace." Suddenly she smiled. It was like the sun coming out from behind a cloud.

From then on, until Chrissy left the train at Johnstown, where her grandmother met her, they talked occasionally. Eddie told about their moving to Pittsburgh and that Pa was the engineer of the train. Girls aren't so bad after all, he thought, wishing Chrissy had been going all the way to Pittsburgh.

At Hollidaysburg there was a rest stop and under the shelter was a counter where food was sold. Everyone chose something from the homemade dishes of potato salad, sandwiches, pickled hard-cooked eggs, cakes, and pies. The men laughed and talked and offered food to Eddie. Pa was still going over the engine to make sure everything was working, for there was to be a test of its strength and ability ahead over the Allegheny Mountains.

Eddie hoped Pa would be too busy to notice him and remember that he hadn't been ready to board the train when the whistle blew. But just as he took his last bite, Pa was there beside him, speaking in the way Eddie knew well. He was out of patience.

"Well! That was a fine thing for you to do after all the trouble we had! Didn't you even *think* about what I have told you? Where were you, eh?"

"Oh, Pa, I'm so sorry! I thought you were all so busy that it would take much longer, and I wanted to see what was in the woods—and I saw Indians!" Eddie couldn't help his eyes shining when he said it. "Indians!"

"But don't you know that you were almost left behind?" Pa frowned at Eddie for a moment, but seeing his excitement and remembering his own first experience in seeing Indians, he began to smile instead.

"Just don't let it happen again!" he said, putting his arm around Eddie's shoulder and guiding him back to the train.

Another man boarded the train, waving farewell to the people watching. Mr. Stewart blew the whistle, Pa rang the bell, and the chuff-chuffing of the alternating pistons began.

It was late afternoon. Eddie was tired and hungry. When would they be in Pittsburgh?

Between Hollidaysburg and Johnstown the mountains really closed in. Eddie, looking out of the window, could hardly see the sky, the mountain rose so steep beside the train. It was terrify-

ing and wonderful. Where would it end? Then the train rounded a curve and came into the open, where Pa slowed up and men attached a cable to the engine and drew it up, by means of a stationary engine, to the top of the mountain. There, Pa stopped again while the cable was transferred to the back of the train. Eddie wondered just how they connected it but overheard the men across the aisle discussing it. One of them said:

"They attach the cable to the coupling. Let's hope that all the couplings hold! Otherwise we'll go headlong, faster and faster, after that little iron horse up front!" He laughed but made a gesture as if in doubt. (Eddie thought, They don't really know how smart Pa is. *He* knows how to use the brakes.)

The cable held and was detached at the foot of the mountain, and soon they were on their way again, turning often to avoid the steep places, sometimes going round and round, rising higher and higher. Eddie could feel the pull of the engine on the rising road. At the top of the rise, the land spread out in a beautiful pattern of field and forest, farm and village. There were the tops of the trees, houses far below in the valley, people too small to be seen.

Across the valley were more mountains, blue in the distance, and the road kept its winding way down.

Eddie kept going first to one side of the train then to the other, there were such wonders to see. Once, the train went round such a curve that Eddie could see the engine ahead for just an instant. It was a beautiful day with fair-weather clouds which added to Eddie's excitement. I can see forever! he thought.

A woman passenger, who had boarded the train at a whistle stop just before the McKeesport Station, opened a package of lunch. She sat right behind Eddie, where the enticing smell of food reminded him that it was several hours since he had eaten. As if the woman had read his mind, she touched his shoulder and said, "Here, boy, aren't you hungry? *I* am." Eddie turned and right there beside his ear was a sandwich, a good healthy sandwich with lots of meat. Eddie took it gratefully, saying:

"Oh, thank you, thank you, ma'am." The woman smiled and somehow made him think of Ma and of Vinny. Where was Vinny? Had she gone to that boarding school where her friends were? When would they get to Pittsburgh?

The train slowed down and stopped at several taverns and stations along the way for rest and food and to take on and discharge passengers. It seemed to Eddie that they would never arrive at Pittsburgh.

The day was almost spent, when Pa finally drew into the station at Pittsburgh. Crowds of people awaited their arrival, waving hanker-chiefs, flags, and banners. Along with the chorus of voices was a burst of music from a brass band. It was a glorious reception to the crew, who had successfully traversed the mountains and valleys from Philadelphia across Pennsylvania to Pittsburgh!

Aunt Sally was among the first ones to greet Pa and immediately took Eddie under her care, while Pa was congratulated by the officials of the Pennsylvania Railroad and invited to join them later at a celebration dinner.

When the commotion had somewhat settled down, Pa attended to ordering the delivery of the household goods which were to be stored in Aunt Sally's barn for the present. Eddie wanted to explore the new station and was eager to see what Pittsburgh was like, but he was tired and sleepy and even Pa yawned as they drove along to Aunt Sally's in the surrey.

"I know how tired you must be," she said, lifting the reins to urge the horse on. "But supper will help. I have it all ready to put on the table. There will be two or three of the boarders with us who will want to hear all about the journey, but don't feel you must answer all their questions. They will understand. They are hard workers too."

During the next few days, Eddie had many new experiences. He and Pa settled into their room at Aunt Sally's, and he found Aunt Sally's cooking very good indeed.

He was entered at the school which was not far away. It was much larger than the Dame school back home, with several classrooms and a number of teachers. He was a little shy at meeting so many new boys and girls. But when they discovered that he was the son of Edward T. Moore, who had driven the first engine from Philadelphia, he became quite popular. The boys wanted to know all the details of the journey. At recess several boys came toward Eddie.

"How long did it take? My name's John. What's yours?" asked a boy about Eddie's age. And without waiting for an answer, "Hey—what's the engine like inside? How does your Pa make it go?"

"Eddie," said Eddie, grinning, because he knew just how eager anybody would be to hear about it. "It took three days and two nights," he went on, as other boys gathered around to hear. The girls hung back a little.

"Pa let me ride with him part of the way, and I saw how he kept hold of the throttle and how he used the brake and rang the bell for a warning and blew the whistle for the crossings. The conductor, Mr. Stewart, was the one who said when to stop and go, but my Pa ran the engine," he finished proudly.

Eddie liked his new teacher, Miss Ellen Latham. She was kind and helpful and was as pretty as Miss Ashton, who had been his teacher at Dame school. There were several subjects new to Eddie—music, botany, and drawing. The music—"Do, re, mi—" was difficult, and he couldn't understand how a song with B♭ was in the key of F. He liked the drawing, of course. Miss Latham said, "You are doing well in art, but in drawing for botany, your drawings are too naturalistic. They should be very simple and clear for this purpose."

Before Christmas, there was an evening meeting for parents and pupils of the upper grades of grammar school. It was a gay party with cakes and lemonade, allowing teachers and parents to meet and discuss the subjects taught and to see how well each pupil was getting along.

Eddie couldn't wait to introduce Pa to Miss Ellen Latham, his teacher. He knew Pa liked her when they met by the way Pa smiled and was pleased when she told how well Eddie was doing in school.

"Yes," she said, "he works hard at learning the principles of music and finds it somewhat difficult, but his drawing is excellent." Then she went on, "I hear you are one of the best engineers in the country!"

Pa smiled again. "I have been as fortunate in having good teachers as Eddie has," he said, laughing.

Yes, Eddie thought to himself, Pa likes her, too.

MARGUERITE DE ANGELI was born on March 14, 1889, in Lapeer, Michigan. Since her first children's story appeared in 1936, she has written over twenty books for young readers which have won her a large and faithful audience and many top awards as well. In 1946 *Bright April* was named an Honor Book by the New York *Herald Tribune*. In 1950, *The Door in the Wall* earned the Newbery Medal, and in 1961 it won a Lewis Carroll Shelf Award. In 1968 Mrs. de Angeli was awarded the Regina Medal by the Catholic Library Association for excellence in writing for young people, and in 1976 she was honored with a Doctor of Letters by Lehigh University. A mother of five, a grandmother of thirteen, and great-grandmother of three, Mrs. de Angeli has found her own family to be a vital source of her special insight into the imagination of children; each of her books reflects the wisdom and personal warmth that have earned her a special place in the hearts of generations of young readers.

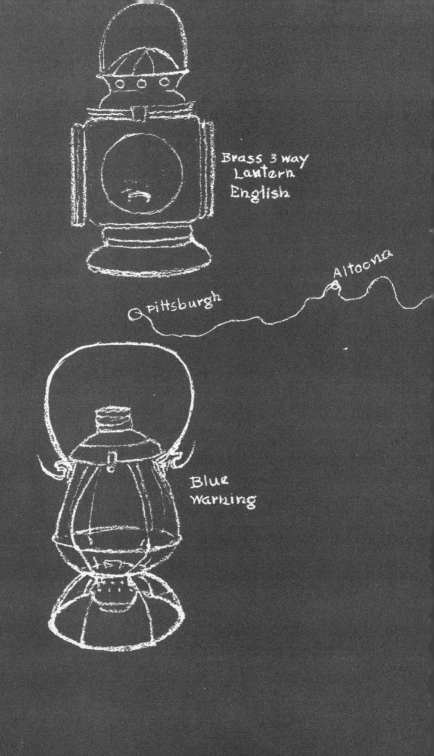

Brass 3 way
Lantern
English

Altoona

Pittsburgh

Blue
Warning